SUE PICKFORD is a British artist of Hong Kong Chinese origin.
She specialised in Illustration for her Higher Diploma in Advertising,
and worked as an Art Director in the advertising industry for ten years.
She is now a creative manager, while also writing and illustrating children's
books. Her first picture book for Frances Lincoln was *Bob and Rob*.
Sue lives with her husband and rescue moggy in Dorset.

My special things

Cosmic cupcakes

Zog the droid dog

flying dusters

Space rainbows

by Angus aged 6½ million light years.

skater wellies

twinkly trousers

robot watering can

For Mum,
Dad, John, Mo
and Richard

JANETTA OTTER-BARRY BOOKS

Text and illustrations copyright © Sue Pickford 2014

The right of Sue Pickford to be identified as the Author and Illustrator of this Work has been asserted by her in accordance with the Copyright, Designs and Patents Act, 1988 (United Kingdom).

First published in Great Britain and in the USA in 2014 by
Frances Lincoln Children's Books,
74-77 White Lion Street, London N1 9PF
www.franceslincoln.com

This paperback edition first published in Great Britain in 2014

A catalogue record for this book is available from the British Library.

ISBN 978-1-84780-524-9

Illustrated with pencil, acrylic and digital media

Printed in China

9 8 7 6 5 4 3 2 1

WHEN ANGUS MET ALVIN

SUE PICKFORD

F

FRANCES LINCOLN
CHILDREN'S BOOKS

Angus was not
the usual sort of alien.

He didn't eat Gruntazorg kebabs,

rockets made his ears **ring**

and laser guns scared him silly.

In fact, what he enjoyed best
in the **whole** universe
was being in his garden
where it was nice and quiet.

One day,
while Angus was hanging
out the washing,
a *strange* spaceship

Crashed

right in the middle
of his lawn
and made the most

monstrous mess!

When the dust settled, the door creaked open…

and another alien jumped out.

"Hi, I'm Alvin!" he announced.

"I've come to show you my special space skills."

"I'd rather you had some cleaning-up skills,"
replied Angus crossly, looking at his ruined garden.

"Well,
so
can I,"
said Angus.

"Look,
I can
fly!"
bragged Alvin.

"Pah, BORING!" scoffed Alvin.

"Now this is what you call skill!"

He switched on his jet boots and started whizzing

round and round and upside down.

"STOP!"

yelled Angus, as twigs and leaves went everywhere.

But Alvin couldn't hear him over the racket.

"See?" he laughed, landing with a THUD.

"Now do something else, go on."

So Angus twisted his ears.
Once to the left
and twice to the right.

Suddenly, a huge tuft of
pink feathers came
sprouting
out of his head.

But Alvin twisted his own
ears until so many feathers
grew, you could hardly see
him underneath them all!

But **that** wasn't
the end of it,
oh no.

He then did

a dozen cartwheels

and pulverised

ALL

the prize pansies.

"Ta-daaaa!"

Right now Angus wished that he could teletransport Alvin to a *faraway* place, but he didn't have the **faintest** clue how.

BY PROFESSOR POPPEMOFF

101 WAYS tO GET RiD OF ANNOYING ALiENS

Then he had an idea!

"Hey Alvin, I bet you can't do this!"
Holding his breath,
Angus jumped on the spot

with his arms stretched right up
until he started to blow up
like a balloon.

He got bigger and **fatter** and **rounder**

until he was **SO** big

he was touching the clouds.

"Pah!"
shouted Alvin.
**"I can do that
juggling
four banamaz
at the same
time."**

So he did,
and he got **bigger**
and **fatter** and **rounder**.

In fact, he got a *million* times
bigger and **fatter** and
rounder until...

and all the air came

whooooshing out,

making him shrink

to the size of a thumb.

Finally he bounced right back into Angus's garden.

"I suppose you think this is funny?" squeaked Alvin.

He fell into a bowl of soup that belonged to Mrs Evans from Number Eleven, Ensbury Avenue, Earth, before bouncing off

into a

GRUNTAZORG'S nest.

"**Listen**," said Angus, trying not to laugh. "I've got some magic stardust that will get you back to normal. But it will only work if you behave yourself."

"**Behaving is another one of my special skills!**" piped teeny-weeny Alvin.

So Angus sprinkled the magic stardust onto Alvin.

Without any further hesitation Alvin offered to make tea. He laid the table – and immediately grew to the size of **a hamster**.

He baked a cosmic cake – and grew to the size of a **hedgehog**.

He made banamaz sandwiches – and grew to the size of a **hound**.

Finally, he poured the tea – and soon he was completely back to Alvin-size again.

To celebrate, Angus
and Alvin sat down
together and ate every
delicious morsel,
washed down
with lots of tea.

Suddenly, Alvin looked at his intergalactic timepiece. **"Oh no!"** he gasped. **"I've got to go, my mum will go bonkers if I'm late...**

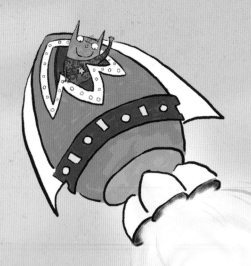

I'll be back when I have
more special skills
to show you.
See you soon!"

And he whizzed away,
waving to his new friend.

"Not too soon, I hope," smiled Angus,
as he settled back into the peace and quiet
of his garden.

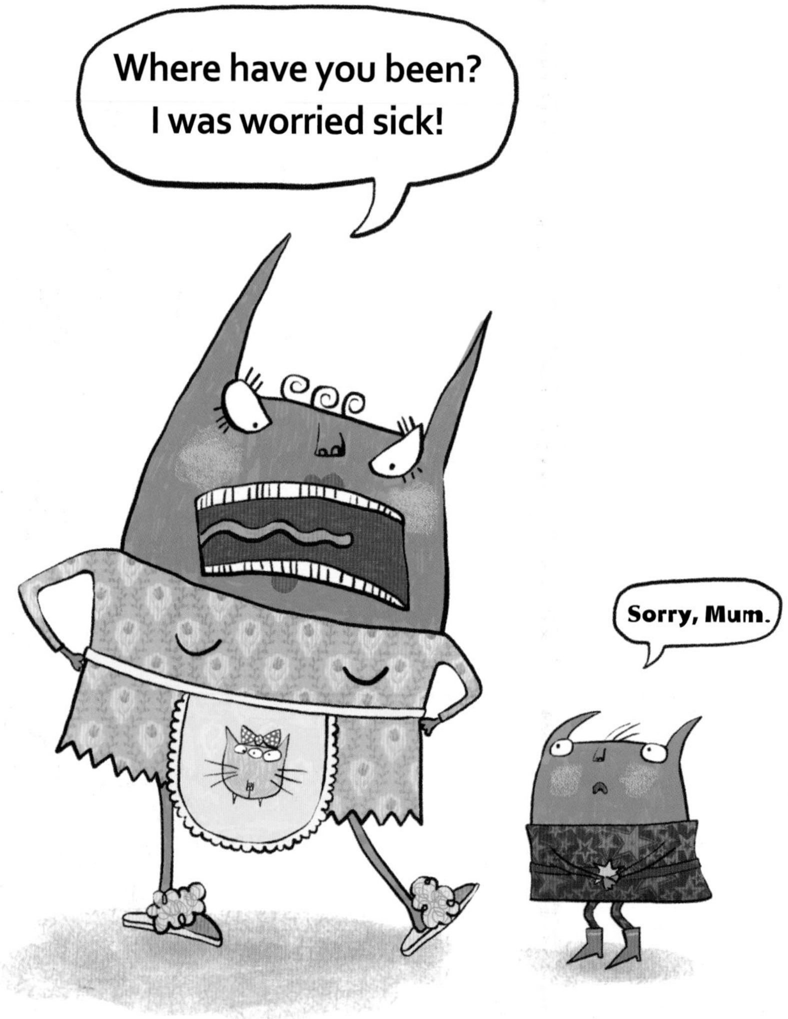
Where have you been?
I was worried sick!
Sorry, Mum.

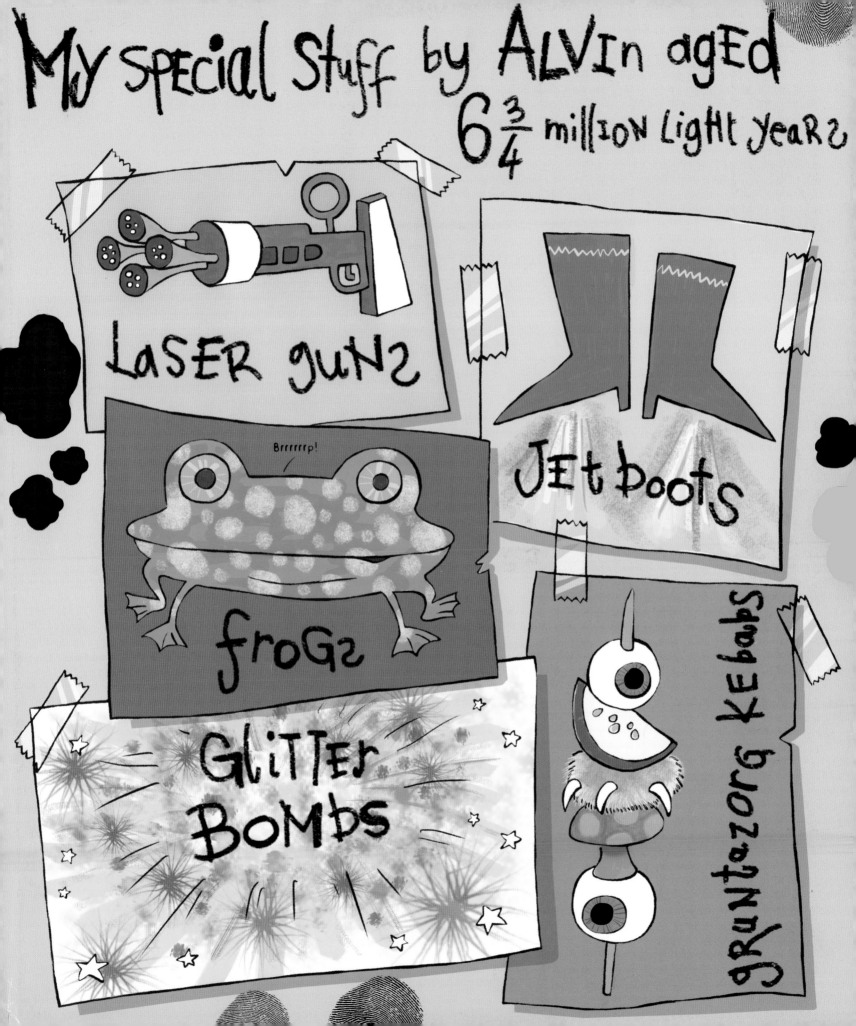

ALSO BY SUE PICKFORD
PUBLISHED BY FRANCES LINCOLN CHILDREN'S BOOKS

BOB AND ROB

"Rob is more bungler than burglar, with a virtuous dog named Bob,
and Sue Pickford writes with gumption about this contrasting pair…
a robust, entertaining moral tale that confirms that even a dog's life
is likely to turn out better than a thief's!" – *Kate Kellaway, Observer*

"Wackily illustrated in comic style, with bold, bright colours, Sue Pickford's
promising debut picture book should win many young friends." – *Books for Keeps*

978-1-84780-343-6

Frances Lincoln titles are available from all good bookshops.
You can also buy books and find out more about your favourite titles,
authors and illustrators on our website: www.franceslincoln.com